Remember Me

One confessional scene (pp. 40-46) when Dan-Marie's
confusion of mediocrity is topped by Lue's obsession about
Lue's self-indulgent self-pity, is best in play. But Lue's
doesn't work.

Obviously, these are moments of honesty
which are moving; but his because
not craft, more because their actual
world is unknown. The shallowness of
Artist reality. The work has life does not, however, have
a superficiality. It persistent ennui and credo
likes. Lack of genuinity, of Ceciirette.
answers often from questions—
stiffness, clumsy—
transitory, tired ideas
immorality of
if ...

REMEMBER ME

**a play by Michel Tremblay
translated by John Stowe**

Talonbooks • Vancouver • 1984

copyright © 1981 Les Editions Leméac Inc.
translation copyright © 1984 John Stowe

published with assistance from the Canada Council

Talonbooks
201 1019 East Cordova Street
Vancouver
British Columbia V6A 1M8
Canada

This book was typeset by Resistance Graphics and printed in
Canada by Hignell Printing Ltd.

First printing: November 1984

Rights to produce *Remember Me*, in whole or in part, in any
medium by any group, amateur or professional, are retained
by the author and interested persons are requested to apply
to his agent, John Goodwin, 4235 avenue de l'Esplanade,
Montreal, Quebec H2W 1T1.

First published by Les Editions Leméac Inc., Montreal,
Quebec. Published by arrangement with Les Editions
Leméac Inc.

Canadian Cataloguing in Publication Data

Tremblay, Michel, 1942-
    Les anciennes odeurs. English
    Remember me

    Translation of: Les anciennes odeurs.
    ISBN 0-88922-219-3

    I. Title. II. Title: Les anciennes odeurs. English.
PS8539.R47A13 1984   C842'.54   C84-091542-X
PQ3919.2.T73A813 1984

Les anciennes odeurs was first performed at Theatre de Quat'Sous in Montreal, Quebec on November 4, 1981, with the following cast:

Jean-Marc   Gilles Renaud
Luc   Hubert Gagnon

Directed by Andre Brassard
Set Design and Costume Design by Francois Laplante

Remember Me was first performed in English by the MTC Warehouse Theatre at the Manitoba Theatre Centre in Winnipeg, Manitoba, on January 11, 1984, with the following cast:

Jean-Marc   Allan Gray
Luc   John Moffat

Directed by Per Brask
Set Design and Costume Design by William Chesney

CHARACTERS

JEAN-MARC, *a French teacher, 38 years old.*
LUC, *an actor, 32 years old.*

Basement converted into a study. JEAN-MARC is sitting at his desk, marking student papers. He is smoking a pipe.

JEAN-MARC:
Two mistakes in the title alone! . . . Incredible.

He counts the remaining papers.

Eleven! There's no end to it.

He looks at his watch.

And it's not even late!

He sighs and goes back to marking his paper. LUC enters slowly and looks around. He sniffs at the smell of tobacco.

LUC:
It always smells the same here. Pipe tobacco, records, and Gentleman by Givenchy.

JEAN-MARC doesn't budge.

JEAN-MARC:
My goodness, a ghost! I didn't hear you ring.

LUC:

I saw Natasha when I went by the kitchen. She didn't look too thrilled to see me.

JEAN-MARC:

Stop calling him Natasha. You know he doesn't like it.

LUC:

Calling him by his real name wouldn't make him any happier.

JEAN-MARC:

So you're still using your key. You didn't ring.

LUC:

I've had the key to this house for seven years. I don't know why I shouldn't use it.

He smiles.

If you don't want me to, change the lock!

JEAN-MARC shakes his head and smiles.

And you can tell . . . what did you say his name was? . . . Guy? Paul? Anyway, you can tell him that when you're not here, I don't come sniffing your sheets to see what you've been up to the night before . . . 'cause that's probably what he thinks!

JEAN-MARC:

For God's sake, Luc . . .

LUC:

I'm sure he'd prefer I didn't exist. After all, he's my replacement, isn't he?

JEAN-MARC:

Whenever you come here, you act like we still lived together. He doesn't like that, what do you expect?

LUC:
>We viewed this house together, we fell in love with it together, we bought it together, we lived in it together for four years . . . and now I'm supposed to ring before I enter?

JEAN-MARC:
>What's past is past, Luc.

LUC:

>My God, you're profound.

>*JEAN-MARC smiles.*

JEAN-MARC:
>What I'm trying to say is that as far as Paul's concerned you're a guest in this house.

LUC:

>Am I a guest as far as you're concerned, too?

>*Short silence.*

JEAN-MARC:
>Yes.

>*LUC rushes out of the room. We hear him run upstairs, cross the house, open a door and close it again.*
>*The doorbell rings.*
>*JEAN-MARC, meanwhile, has gone back to marking his papers, laughing to himself.*
>*LUC comes back in slowly and sits down in a large, worn-out leather armchair.*

You'd really like him to despise you, is that it?

LUC:

>He's got no sense of humour. If he did, he'd adore me.

JEAN-MARC:

> You know something? He's not the only one who
> doesn't understand your sense of humour.

LUC:

> Look, I'm not kidding, he had an apron around his
> waist!

> *JEAN-MARC frowns then smiles.*

JEAN-MARC:

> I don't think *you* understand *his* sense of humour.

LUC:

> Him? My God, when he cracks a joke, I feel like
> burying my head under a pillow.

JEAN-MARC:

> When you arrived, did he have an apron around his
> waist?

LUC:

> I don't know, I didn't notice.

JEAN-MARC:

> Precisely! If he'd had one, you'd have noticed.

> *Short silence. LUC smiles.*

LUC:

> Okay. A point for him. The first in a donkey's age,
> mind you.

> *Silence.*

> If it had been me, though, at least I'd have had
> "Natasha" embroidered in the corner!

> *They laugh quietly together.*

> Are you marking papers?

JEAN-MARC:
What kind of dumb question is that? Can't you see?

LUC:
It's not a dumb question. It's an attempt at
conversation.

JEAN-MARC:
I'm working, Luc, and it's a pain in the ass, but I've
got to finish it tonight. Anyway, you can talk to me
while I'm marking, you always did and it never
bothered me.

LUC:

It's true, you know, it always smells the same. . . .
Whenever I come here—into the study, that is, since
the bedroom is now forbidden territory—I breathe in,
and all these images are conjured up. . . .

> *Silence.*

I don't know why the past always smells so good.

> *Silence. He looks toward JEAN-MARC.*

Can you smell me when I come here?

JEAN-MARC:
You haven't changed your cologne since we've known
each other, Luc. Of course I can smell you.

LUC:
And it doesn't make you feel weird?

JEAN-MARC:
What's the point . . .?

LUC:

Can you smell it, right now?

JEAN-MARC:
> Of course.

> *LUC smiles.*

LUC:
> Knowing you, you'll say it doesn't remind you of
> happy memories.

JEAN-MARC:
> What really amazes me is that my cologne seems to
> remind you of nothing but happy memories.

LUC:

> On the contrary, it doesn't just remind me of happy
> memories. I said that the *past* smelled good . . . which
> is not the same. The past in general.

JEAN-MARC:
> And the present?

LUC:

> Not so fast! You'll have to wait a bit. It'll come soon
> enough.

> *JEAN-MARC puts down his papers.*

> These days I often think of the evenings I spent here,
> in this chair, learning my lines while you were
> working. . . . My God . . . the peace. . . .

JEAN-MARC:
> You left because you found it *too* peaceful . . . and
> because you felt you were being buried alive.

LUC:

I know. But that's not what I'm talking about. And I'm not saying that I regret leaving. It's just that . . . if anyone asked me what was the happiest moment of my life, I'd say it was the time when we were rehearsing the de Musset play, at the Theatre School, and I was having one helluva time with my lines. Remember, with my "t"'s and "d"'s: "How devastating to be ridiculed in a tête à tête, or teased at a dinner party."

JEAN-MARC:

Well, at least you don't have that problem now. Not with what you're playing these days. . . .

LUC: *ironically*

You're wrong, my friend. To celebrate the tenth anniversary of our so-called artistic careers, a gang of us from my year at school have decided to remount "Le Chandelier."

JEAN-MARC:

Don't tell me you want to play Fortunio at your age!

LUC gets up and turns toward JEAN-MARC.

LUC:

Touché! Heed this magnificent wound, this splendid dagger. Heed the blood which floweth. . . .

JEAN-MARC smiles.

JEAN-MARC:

At least it's not in your back, you can always pull it out.

LUC:

We're putting it on at the Quat'Sous. It should work.

13

JEAN-MARC:

> It'll be a big shock for your fans, though. They're so used to seeing you play that dummy on television.

> *LUC turns his back to JEAN-MARC.*

LUC:

> Bullseye! Congratulations! Right between the shoulder-blades!

JEAN-MARC:

> Sorry.

LUC:

> You don't have to be sorry. I know what you think about all that. You're not the only one.

JEAN-MARC:

> And you . . . what do you think about it?

LUC:

> How can I think about it, I'm in it! Anyway, I'm satisfied just to earn my living. When you make compromises as major as that, you try not to think about it.

JEAN-MARC:

> Is that what you came to talk about?

LUC:

> Come on! You're not my father confessor, as far as I know!

> *They look at each other and smile.*

> My God! The same old words.

JEAN-MARC:

> The same old tone.

LUC:

>The same old place.

>>*They laugh.*
>>*JEAN-MARC draws close to LUC and takes him in*
>>*his arms.*

JEAN-MARC:

>Hi, Luc.

LUC:

>Hi.

JEAN-MARC:

>How are things?

LUC:

>Pretty bad.

>>*JEAN-MARC leaves hold of LUC, and LUC sits*
>>*down in his chair.*

JEAN-MARC:

>Is it your father?

LUC:

>Yes.

JEAN-MARC:

>Will it be long?

LUC:

>A few days at the most.

JEAN-MARC:

>He's still conscious?

LUC:

>Yes. He wants to see you. That's why I came. He told
>me he wanted to speak to you.

JEAN-MARC:

> He knows we're no longer together. . . .

LUC:

> You know very well, Jean-Marc, officially he never
> knew we were together. That is, he knew, but he
> didn't want to know. . . . His beloved son's best friend
> . . . the inseparable twosome. . . . But he likes you a
> lot and I think he wants to say goodbye.

JEAN-MARC:

> We haven't seen each other for ages. I wouldn't know
> what to say to him.

LUC:

> You think I know what to say to him? For two months
> now, I've been watching him die, every evening, for
> three hours. . . . He'll only be conscious a few more
> days, Jean-Marc. Surely you could do that for him.
> There's hardly anything I can say any more. I've
> exhausted all possible topics of conversation: I talked
> about the house, the family, the weather, the TV, the
> traffic on Gouin Boulevard, the food at the hospital.
> . . . And all the while he just sits there, staring out the
> window at Bordeaux prison. He doesn't even answer
> me any more, doesn't even listen to my jokes—God
> knows they're getting fewer and fewer, and worse than
> ever. . . . I was so naive: I wanted him to die with a
> smile on his face, not knowing what was happening,
> while I'd be telling him a story, or fussing around his
> bedside imitating my Aunt Blondine whom he always
> hated, or my Uncle Hector who died of exhaustion
> during a face-pulling marathon at his daughter's
> wedding.

> *Silence.*

> He keeps straightening the sheets, smoothing out the
> creases, looking out the window.

Silence.

The day I drove him back to Notre Dame de la Merci, he got into bed all by himself, looked out the window, and said: "Last thing I'm gonna see before I die, are those damn prison walls!"

Silence.

Sometimes I sit there and watch him suffer. . . . I see him suffering when he forces a smile, and want to say to him: "Die, will you!" "Please! Die! I'll help you! I'll hold your hand. . . . I'll lead you there, just die!" When he starts thrashing about in the bed and I have to call the nurse to give him an injection, it's humiliating for him and I can't help crying . . . and he hates it when I cry.

Silence.

A few days after he arrived at the hospital, the doctor told me he'd stopped eating, he could hardly digest anything any more, but when I went back to his room, the first thing he did was order a soup. He said he was hungry! I tried to explain there was no point in forcing himself to eat, but he just got angry and accused me of wanting to stop him from feeding himself. Then when the soup arrived, he was like a dog—a beaten, worn-out dog. He kept looking at me, with his eyes wide open, trying with what little strength he had, to put the spoon in his mouth, as if he were trying to tell me: "Look! I'm still here . . . I'm still eating!" And he was shaking and retching and spilling it everywhere. . . .

Silence.

Imagine someone you've loved so much, admired so much. A dog.

Silence.

Yesterday, a few minutes after his injection, he was
starting to feel better so I told him I had to go because
I had a rehearsal. He asked me to come closer to the
bed and he took my hand. . . . My father. Imagine! I
don't think I'd touched him since I was ten years old!
He whispered to me: "It's hard! If only you knew how
hard. Don't stay to watch. Go!"

Silence. He suddenly gets up.

Christ, the injustice of it all! I wish I could scream! I
wish I could smash the furniture, bash somebody's face
in, throw myself on the ground and pound the floor
with my fists, but I can't. I cry in front of him but I
can't cry when I'm by myself, though my own room is
the best place for it! I could do whatever I like and no
one would ever know! But I get into bed, I lie there,
eyes wide open, and all that happens is that I'm scared
. . . scared of death.

Silence.

Once I saw the nurses change his bed. He's so thin! So
small. Fragile. I remember him sturdy and strong,
always ready to sing us a tune, tell us a story. I
remember him kissing and cuddling my mother, and
she'd always protest, but never stop him, because she
loved every minute of it; I've seen him, in his
workshop, starting up that huge printing press,
watching over it lovingly. . . . When I was a kid I used
to tremble in his arms when we'd fool around together,
and later I trembled even more, when they explained
the Oedipus complex to me at school. . . . That man
has been so much a part of my life. How will I live
without him?

Silence.

When I stand there at his bedside I see my own future
lying there, staring me in the face, and I'm so afraid!
What's the point of struggling so hard if that's where it
leads you?

Silence.

Besides, it stinks!

Silence.

That's all you needed to hear tonight, isn't it? But
you're the only one I can tell it to.

JEAN-MARC: *smiling*
I've always been a good shoulder to cry on. You've
said so many times.

LUC:
It used to drive me mad when people would pour out
their troubles to you . . . like I just did.

JEAN-MARC:
Well, you were never shy about doing it, that's for
sure.

LUC: *smiling*
I had the right. . . .

JEAN-MARC: *ironically*
Because I belonged to you. . . .

LUC: *in the same tone*
For Heaven's sake, let's not start that again.

JEAN-MARC: *after a moment's silence*
What about your brothers? Where have they been all
this time?

LUC:

They don't visit my father because they can't bear to
see him like that. Can you believe that excuse? I'm not
saying they have no feelings. In fact, it looks like
they've got too many. But in the meantime, I'm the
one who shudders, I'm the one who's revolted, when I
see the person I love most in the world suffering such
humiliation! I sit on a chair, back straight, arms
folded, knees together, and I watch him quietly
slipping away, and I curse and swear at the absurdity
of it all.

Silence.

I'm running out of patience.

Silence.

JEAN-MARC:

I don't know what to say. When you're like this no
one can do anything for you. Except listen. Would you
like a drink?

LUC:

You're offering *me* one? I don't drink now any more
than I used to.

JEAN-MARC:

Have you eaten?

LUC:

No. But don't disturb Natasha on my account. I'm not
hungry, anyway.

JEAN-MARC:

I could fix you something quick.

LUC:

> Don't tell me you've learned to cope on your own, I
> don't believe it. You mean you really could make me
> something right now, an omelette or a sandwich that
> wouldn't be completely revolting?

JEAN-MARC:

> Necessity is the mother of invention.

LUC:

> What do you mean, "Necessity is the mother of
> invention"? When you get home from school in the
> evening, isn't Natasha waiting for you lovingly with
> dindins in the oven?

JEAN-MARC: *interrupting him*

> Paul works, Luc. We share the household chores.

LUC:

> Oops! . . . Touché once again. It's true, I wasn't
> working at the time, I was just a poor student, I had
> loads of time to spoil you. But we mustn't forget
> Natasha has a real job! Is that what you were trying to
> say?

JEAN-MARC:

> Not at all!

> *Silence.*

> Well, maybe.

> *They smile.*

LUC:

> These days, let me tell you, I wouldn't have the time
> to spoil you either. I've been running all over the place
> the last six months . . . hardly had time to breathe.
> . . . But perhaps I too, in the end, would have
> managed to train you—like Natasha!

JEAN-MARC:

Luc, please, call him by his proper name!

LUC:

It's funny, there are some people you just can't picture having a real job. I can't picture your lover-boy anywhere but in a kitchen.

JEAN-MARC:

I know you think he's totally useless, Luc, but Jesus Christ!

LUC:

I just can't for the life of me imagine Paul looking after a bunch of screaming brats...

JEAN-MARC:

They're not that young.

LUC:

The last time I came here for dinner, he told me he spends his days changing diapers; you don't call that young? He works in a kindergarten, Jean-Marc, not a primary school, or have you already forgotten? Does this mean you've stopped telling each other the latest office gossip? Or is it the little silence after breakfast? The little heads buried in the morning paper?

They look at each other.
JEAN-MARC is the first to look away.

Do you love him?

JEAN-MARC:

In a way. Not passionately, perhaps. I can't give him that. But he knows it.

LUC:

What about him?

22

JEAN-MARC:

> You mean, does he love me? I think he keeps himself
> from getting too involved because he knows exactly
> where he stands.

LUC   *softly*

> So you still let people love you without giving much in
> return. All your lovers in the past few years have
> suffered for it . . . but you continue. You let them get
> attached to you but never get involved yourself. You
> take advantage of them and one fine day they end up
> realizing it . . . and then you're amazed when they
> make a scene!

JEAN-MARC:

> What are you looking for, justification?

LUC:

> Sometimes I think I understand you . . . but other
> times I find you ridiculous. Go out and screw around,
> Jean-Marc. You're good-looking, you never had
> trouble scoring! Make a whole bunch of people suffer,
> instead of just one at a time!

JEAN-MARC   *pouring out two cognacs*
> Why are you telling me this all of a sudden?

LUC:

> You're always so reasonable . . . so in control . . . at
> least that's the impression you give. But I know it's not
> true, and it drives me crazy.

> *JEAN-MARC goes over and hands LUC a glass.*

JEAN-MARC:

> Have one anyway. It'll do you good.

> *He kneels beside LUC's armchair, sitting on his
> haunches. They start drinking.*

LUC:
Just like the good old days. . . .

JEAN-MARC:
Except that in those days we'd be holding hands.

Silence.

Everything you'd like to feel for your father, but can't;
the anger, the tears, sobbing your heart out, crying
and blowing your nose for weeks and weeks, I did it all
for you, Luc, when you left, and you know it. It's too
soon for you to have forgotten. It took me a long time
to get over it, and even now, it still hurts. It's only
natural I don't want it to start all over again.

Silence.

And I'm not talking about love! I'm talking about
pride! Wounded pride hurts much much longer. When
you've thrown yourself at someone's feet once in your
life, you're in no hurry for it to happen again. You cut
yourself off. You put up barriers. You become more
wary. More reasonable. I'm not unreasonable, Luc.
I've become reasonable. In self-defense. Deep down
I'm basically the faithful type. What can I do? It's not
my fault, it's the way I am. And besides, you can't say
you haven't benefited from it. I like to experience
things with one person at a time. And in fact, the only
time I was ever unreasonable in my feelings was with
you, and I found myself, after seven years, in a heap
on the floor in what used to be our bedroom,
screaming out in despair because I'd just found out
you were cheating on me, right, left, and centre, and I
was the only person in town who didn't know! So, ever
since then I don't trust people. I still have just one
lover at a time, but I don't get so involved. I hope you
can understand.

Silence.

That way, if I find out I've been cheated on again, it won't hurt so much.

Silence.

I've become reasonable.

LUC:
That must be a drag sometimes.

JEAN-MARC:
Is your life really so exciting, Luc?

LUC:
Well, at least I avoid that kind of problem!

Brief silence.

JEAN-MARC:
Did you ever love me?

LUC: *very brusquely*
Yes! Oh, yes! Don't you ever doubt it! I was screwing around all over the place, it's true, I admit that, but I wasn't cheating on you.

JEAN-MARC bursts out laughing.

I tried to explain all that before I left, but you could never understand.

JEAN-MARC:
I still don't.

LUC:
I can distinguish between my feelings and my physical desires, that's all.

JEAN-MARC:
>
> And you're also alone.

LUC:
>
> I'm the one who left, Jean-Marc! If I'd really been the kind of jerk you kept shooting your mouth off about everywhere you went for six months, I would have stayed, and I would have promised never to do it again, even though I was incapable, and I'd have gone on playing my little game. Only this time, I'd have made sure you never found out! And that's when I would have been cheating on you, Jean-Marc! But I loved you too much for that. And nowadays I don't feel like cooling my appetites just so some little fusspot-lover, no matter how good-looking, no matter how intelligent, will be waiting at home for me every night, even if I do need affection. And certainly, I need affection, that's obvious. My bed is cold and empty a lot of the time but at least I'm hurting no one but myself!

JEAN-MARC:
>
> When we first met you never talked like that.

LUC:
>
> I never talked like that because in those days I didn't know myself well enough. I was scared to acknowledge certain needs which I considered ugly because you didn't feel them. You governed my thoughts for seven whole years, Jean-Marc, and believe me I'm grateful, goddamned grateful, because you taught me how to live. I have wings now, and my skies are no longer uniformly blue.

JEAN-MARC: *ironically*
>
> I do believe I detect the style of a certain teacher of French who in days gone by endeavoured to court the Muse. . . .

LUC:

I know when I've been influenced and I admit it, that's all! Speaking of influences, how's your writing?

JEAN-MARC:

If you take my advice, you'll forget the influence.

LUC:

Is it that bad?

JEAN-MARC:

I re-read my latest draft last week, and it was such a downer, you wouldn't believe it. As a French teacher I'm a great success, and like all French teachers, I should be satisfied with my lot.

LUC:

But you were satisfied, weren't you?

JEAN-MARC:

Which only goes to show that my skies are no longer uniformly blue. Sometimes I think you believe I'm much simpler than I really am.

LUC:

I never said you were simple.

JEAN-MARC:

But didn't you think so?

LUC makes no reply, but merely raises his glass to JEAN-MARC's good health.

JEAN-MARC: *after a moment's silence*
Last summer, Paul spent a month in the Gaspé with
his parents. . . . It's funny, even though I don't feel
any great passion for him, I was so lost. I felt all alone,
in this big city, where there's no end of opportunities
to meet people, yet I was completely and utterly
helpless. You remember how I kept moping around all
last August? I spent my entire vacation waiting for
letters and post-cards. I was in a dreadful state! At
thirty-eight!

LUC:
That's neither love nor passion, Jean-Marc, that's
possessiveness. Or stubbornness.

He looks at JEAN-MARC.

mockingly   Or maybe it's not as simple as that?

JEAN-MARC:
I met two or three guys who completely depressed me.
No conversation before, no conversation after, and
during, just grunts and groans, and squeals like pigs
being slaughtered. . . . Somehow I don't find that very
exciting. And when morning rolls around, should the
guy have deigned to spend the night with you, you
throw him out like a used Kleenex; and as soon as he's
out the door, you can't remember his face. In fact, you
remember the big fat vein he had on his prick more
than you remember his face! I'd much rather
concentrate my energy on a body I know by heart, a
body I know how to make come, a body on which I
can linger without being obliged to perform a million
feats, whose smell I can breathe in when we've finished
making love, without finding it suspect. Why is it that
most of the guys you meet want to jump in the shower
thirty seconds after they've ejaculated, just when it's
starting to smell good! Don't laugh, Luc! Every time I
talk to you about it you look at me with that
condescending air and that sarcastic little grin. . . . It's
infuriating!

LUC:

> I can't help it, Jean-Marc. I happen to be one of those guys who takes a shower straight afterwards. And don't forget that when you remember the vein on the guy's prick more than his face, his prick was probably the most interesting thing about him!

JEAN-MARC:

> That's not always true! Not in your case!

LUC:

> How would you know? I'm not the cute little joyboy you used to drag everywhere like your disciple, so proud because he was making this astounding progress thanks to your learned advice and fatherly care! Thanks to you, for seven years, I was passionately interested in things whose existence I wasn't even aware of before I met you. You're a wonderful teacher. You communicate things so skillfully, with such affection; it's because of you, as much as, if not more than my teachers, that I became a good actor. You have this incredible facility for understanding a script instinctively; when you explain it, it's as if we'd always understood it. So when I left here, sighing with relief, chirping with excitement because the little door to my big cage had just been opened, my priorities changed, Jean-Marc, and I became your average slut again, on the lookout for cheap thrills, short and sweet, especially on the sly, because I like the anonymity and probably the danger too. It was very exciting to go back into that darkness you'd hauled me out of, only to tyrannize me with your all-exclusive, suffocating love, and all year long now I spend my time groping in some dark room filled with men who smell strong and breathe heavily, who quiver for a few seconds when you touch them after stuffing up their noses the famous heart-booster, the almighty poppers, the blessed host of the new sexuality, which blows their mind and heightens their virility; guys who dirty you when they come, and turn to the wall when it's over, religiously capping their bottle of miracle-cure that leaves a stale

29

and sickly smell of ill-washed sensual pleasure. I'm not saying it's beautiful. But I don't want you to think it's ugly, either. Because it's what I need. Sometimes it's depressing . . . well, it's often depressing, but I don't think it's ugly. The pleasure you give is violent, the pleasure you take is violent, and afterwards you get down to more serious things.

Silence.

More of the same.

He looks at JEAN-MARC.

There's nothing more boring, Jean-Marc, than forcing yourself to make conversation before and after screwing some guy you have nothing to say to, and you know you'll never see again. The shower's a refuge, an alibi. I can't believe you've never understood that. It's all very well smelling good when you've finished screwing, but it's a drag to have to pretend you're some kind of animal who falls asleep as soon as his head hits the pillow! When I get out of the shower, and I pull back the see-through plastic curtain with some beef-cake drawn on it, unless it's imitation cotton lace or some stupid paisley print, I'm ready to start all over. Already I'm on the lookout for a pair of eyes to send me reeling, a pair of shoulders to set my heart pounding. Before I've even pulled my jeans back on I'm getting all worked up thinking of the next time I'll be having them whipped off me! I fall in love ten times a day, and if some guy doesn't respond to my braying and bellowing, my heart's broken for thirty seconds. I fall into the depths of despair, with this horrible sinking feeling inside! Okay, it doesn't last long, but it happens often, and I don't get over it! I want them all, Jean-Marc! All! While I still can. Before it's too difficult. Before it's no longer possible! I walk down the street, head between my shoulders, peering, gaping, bursting with joy or sinking into unbearable despondency, but I keep going! It's how I leave my mark, my imprint! I keep moving like a river, discharging my refuse into the sea! And any bird that happens to fly over my estuary can't miss the stain I make, the blemish I leave behind me, a floating raft of superb bodies, used once and once only, before I discard them, without even giving them time to dry!

While he is saying all this he gets up and paces up and down behind the armchair.

My God! Why on earth am I telling you all this? It's not exactly the most delicate thing to say to your ex-lover.

JEAN-MARC:

That never stopped you before.

LUC:

I feel as if I'm talking to you like a son to his father . . . once again. It's true . . . when all's said and done, you would have made a good father.

JEAN-MARC:

Don't be mean, Luc. I've got enough problems with that as it is.

LUC:

For once I wasn't trying to be mean. . . . Don't tell me Natasha calls you daddy!

JEAN-MARC:

No. It's not Paul I'm having trouble with, it's at school.

LUC:

Not the freshman follies again! Mind you, now that your hair's turning grey, it must be ten times worse.

JEAN-MARC:

> You noticed, did you? It's terrible, I'm getting greyer every day. . . .

LUC:

> It looks great.

JEAN-MARC:

> Just wait till *you* start.

> > *LUC goes and kneels again by the side of the armchair.*

LUC:

> I already have. You must have noticed. Look!

> > *JEAN-MARC looks through LUC's hair for a few moments.*

JEAN-MARC:

> There's a few here and there but nothing to write home about. It's true, though, it must be worse for a well-known actor than for some obscure college prof.

> > *LUC takes a swig of cognac.*

> And what about me?

LUC:

> What do you mean, what about you?

JEAN-MARC:

> I wouldn't mind another cognac myself . . .

LUC:

> Ughhh! I can't be bothered to get up again! You can drink from mine. For once, you've got a well-known actor at your feet, so make the most of it instead of getting drunk.

JEAN-MARC takes a swig from LUC's glass.

LUC:

So does the poor innocent prof still have dirty young men flocking around him?

JEAN-MARC:

I wish I found it as funny as you do. Some years it gets so far out of hand it scares me! It's getting more and more difficult to be honest about it.

LUC laughs.

JEAN-MARC:

Don't laugh; it's true! I decided a long time ago to always say at the beginning of the year that I'm homosexual; that way there's no possibility of confusion, no one can make any wisecracks if they start suspecting things. . . . The first few years, it always shocked them, to begin with, but they didn't talk much about it and there were always a few shy ones, who'd come and tell me their problems after a month or two. . . . But now, the word's got around and everyone's expecting it, so that during the first class, just when I'm about to spring it on them, there's always some smart-ass who says: "We know you're a faggot!" or some such crack. I feel like one of those ancient profs who tells the same old jokes every year at the same time, and the students sit there, just waiting to make him look like an idiot. And what's more, I don't know if it's the in thing, or if people are just getting to be less hung up about it, but as soon as classes start, suddenly there's a bunch of superb young guys and ravishing young girls throwing themselves at me, bombarding me with questions, not to mention other things! Some are clearly not interested but want to know how come it exists; others might be interested but just for a try; and there are those who are definitely interested and begging for it! I decided a long time ago never to get involved with a student, it would be far too complicated. But let me tell you, it's bloody hard! 'Cause when they want to they really want to! They remind me of grade one kids taking an apple to teacher, only they're not in grade one and it's no apple! Eighteen- or nineteen-year-olds, when they put their minds to it, can be so fucking gorgeous. Trying to resist them is agony. They discover the art of seduction, then they try it out on me! Sometimes I actually have to tell them to watch out, I'm not a block of wood, but it's no use. They give me these big sorrowful looks, as if I'm their big bad daddy who's just scolded them. Besides playing the teacher who's trying to interest them in a subject that makes them want to throw up, I have to play the understanding father who's got a solution for everything! Even their heartaches. They come and discuss their love life, and make big cow eyes at me. One guy even brought his girlfriend to me so I could explain his problem to her—he couldn't talk about it on his own—and he ended up confessing that he'd been in love with me since the beginning of the year. I don't know if he was putting me on or what. I even wonder if he hadn't set it up with his girlfriend in advance. You end up so paranoid, it's not funny!

LUC laughs.

Must sound funny to hear it like that, but just try it, my friend, and see what you think! I turn around to write something on the board; next thing I know, I'm getting wolf-whistles at my back. I stay cool, I ask who did it, and all the guys raise their hands!

He takes another swig from LUC's glass.

Some of them have real problems and I do my best to help them out, but others just want to flirt, and they're usually the best-looking.

LUC:

> Make the most of it! Go for it!

JEAN-MARC:

> I don't want to! If I start that, I'll never see the end of it. . . .

LUC:

> So much the better.

JEAN-MARC:

> It's complicated enough as it is, trying to cope with twenty-five rowdy students who aren't the least bit interested in what you're telling them. To start screwing around on top of that. . . .

LUC:

> Must be frustrating. . . .

JEAN-MARC: *interrupting him*

> Of course it is, but what do you expect? I stand by my principles, even though I know it's ridiculous.

LUC:

> That's not what I meant. What I meant was that it must be frustrating having to leave behind all those scrumptious-looking kids, only to end up here in Natasha's arms. . . .

> > *They laugh.*

JEAN-MARC:

> Paul is very handsome, I'll have you know.

LUC:

> Handsome! When he holds out his hand I feel as if I'm standing in front of a glass door. I have this urge to push him against the wall so that people won't bang into him! He's transparent, insipid, gormless; but alas, not odourless.

JEAN-MARC:

Aha! So he smells now, does he?

LUC:

Oh, we all know you're blinded by him, no wonder you can't smell him either! When he comes anywhere near me I get such a whiff of camphor it makes me nauseous.

JEAN-MARC:

You're exaggerating!

LUC:

Damn right I'm exaggerating. It's not camphor he smells of, it's wintergreen! Which is worse! If you're in the process of educating him the way you did me ten years ago, you could at least teach him how to use his perfume.

JEAN-MARC:

I'm not in the process of educating him.

LUC:

Jean-Marc! You educate everyone you meet! Even taxi drivers! You can't help it. The day you were born you were showing people how to live their lives, and you'll go on telling people what to do until the day you die. It's all very well to complain about being chased by naughty students but deep down, you love it! You're a true educator and anything connected with other people's problems—their groping, struggling, questioning, their letdowns, their hopes, their despair—it all interests you passionately! In fact, it's your main reason for living! And the day your students stop chasing after you and asking for advice, or anything else for that matter, you'll droop like a wet rag, and start feeling old and unwanted! Deep down, you want to belong to the whole world! You don't need to fuck all the guys you meet to cheat on your lover. There are more subtle ways of doing it.

36

JEAN-MARC:

>You say that because all the time we were together you were jealous of the attention I paid to my students.

LUC:

>I said it because you were only just speaking about honesty, Jean-Marc. And if, for you, honesty only ends the moment you put your hand on any guy's ass, apart from your lover's, well, I find your idea of honesty a bit elastic.

JEAN-MARC:

>I can hardly not find them attractive when they really are.

LUC:

>Of course not; I know! But for Christ's sake, stop playing the hero.

JEAN-MARC:

>I'm not playing the hero!

LUC:

>Remember when you fell in love with that little creep Lemieux?

JEAN-MARC:

>Oh God, here we go again. . . .

LUC:

>Yes, *that* again! It's a perfect example. You were in love with that guy for a whole semester; you couldn't sleep, you kept crying to yourself in some corner, and I couldn't figure out what to do because I felt abandoned. . . . You never actually fucked him, but all the time you wanted him you were cheating on me, Jean-Marc, just as I was cheating on you whenever I got laid, by anyone, the way I used to. . . .

>*JEAN-MARC gets up suddenly.*

JEAN-MARC:

> At least I tried to fight it! Give me that. At least I
> respected you enough to tell you everything, and hope
> that you'd understand, because I knew in the end it
> would pass. Honesty doesn't stop the moment you put
> your hand on some guy's ass. Honesty ends when you
> hide it from your lover. And I never hid anything from
> you, Luc.

LUC:

> If I hid things from you, it's because you weren't
> ready for them. And maybe I couldn't explain them
> since I didn't really understand them myself. It's hard,
> you know, to admit that you're falling deeper and
> deeper into what your lover calls "adolescent
> sexuality", while he's sitting there screwing up his face
> like some prissy little virgin. My activities would have
> scandalized you and your precious principles, so I
> ended up pretending I was hardly aware of the shrubs
> in public parks, or the bushes on Mount Royal when
> in fact that's where I spent a great deal of my energy.
> And when I found myself after so many years playing
> "Show me your dick" again in a group, in a gang, in
> a crowd, in a horde—and in vain, because afterwards
> you feel really alone—I felt like a boy scout who thanks
> to his group leader has just discovered his penis is for
> more than just having a pee, and . . . well, I wasn't
> ashamed, but I did feel very adolescent, so I said to
> myself: "Sonuvabitch, he's right again!" But I loved
> it; it excited me! And I still love it; and it still excites
> me! And if I didn't tell you at the time, maybe it's
> because in my own way I too was being honest.

JEAN-MARC:

> You waited till some charitable soul who recognized
> you in the dark came and told me. If I hadn't found
> out at the time, Luc, would you still be with me today,
> hiding it?

38

LUC:

> Christ, sometimes I doubt your intelligence, Jean-
> Marc, though I know you're not stupid. I left for other
> reasons too. Mainly to prove to myself that I could live
> without a guardian. Do you realize how suffocating
> you are to live with, Jean-Marc? I couldn't go on like
> that, living in your shadow; you'd been my mentor
> long enough. I needed to fly with my own wings. And
> whatever the outcome, at least I've done it on my own!

> *He looks up at the ceiling.*

> I don't know why all of a sudden I get the feeling that
> Natasha's up there in the living-room, his ear glued to
> the floor, listening to what we're saying. . . .

JEAN-MARC: *smiling*

> Now that's what I call projection. You, you're the one
> who would do that.

LUC:

> It's true. My God! You know me so well, it scares me!
> Me? Spy on you? All that time we were together. You
> better believe it! It's so funny when I think about it.

JEAN-MARC:

> So you're the one who was screwing around, while
> keeping an eye on me, hoping to catch me out.

LUC:

> I wasn't hoping to catch you out.

JEAN-MARC:

> Luc! Come on! If you'd been able to catch me out, things would have been so much easier! You used to go through my pockets looking for bits of paper with names and telephone numbers; when you'd come home late you'd check all the ashtrays because I smoke a pipe and you don't smoke at all; if I left without telling you where I was going you'd follow me. If you'd discovered me with some other guy, Luc, you'd probably have dropped me on the spot, without ever telling me what you'd been up to for years and years!

LUC:

> Just because you consider yourself honest, is no reason to assume everybody around you is dishonest!

JEAN-MARC:

> You're right. I'm sorry. I didn't realize what I was saying.

LUC:

> I hope not!

> *JEAN-MARC comes and kneels down in front of LUC.*

JEAN-MARC:

> At any rate, first of all I must be honest with myself. Only these days it's tough. Not long ago, I realized something that's very hard for me to accept. . . . When you arrived, you were talking to me about my writing. . . . When I re-read that unspeakable thing I dare call my novel. . . . How can I say it? It's the first time I've tried to put it into words. I read it over again, from beginning to end. It's neat, it's well written—that's the very least it should be, I teach French, after all—it's relatively well constructed, but it's painfully and unbelievably boring! You never used to comment very much on what I was writing, Luc.

You'd read it, and you'd tell me it was interesting. What a godawful word. Interesting! What on earth does it mean? Interesting? But you were right. Even if you want to be very very generous, there's not a helluva lot you can say. Because it has absolutely no guts whatsoever. It's as simple as that! I have no guts, Luc, and that's really hard to take when you have pretensions of being a writer. That's what the different publishers I've approached have always tried to make me understand, politely: what I write is utterly boring and, more than that, utterly useless. It never gets off the ground. It says what it has to say, but it says very little. If only you knew how hard that is . . . to be a nobody. When you wanted to change the world. When you write it's because you hope you can change something in the world, Luc. But when your greatest achievement is to bore people to death, because your work is gutless, you should have the intelligence to acknowledge it, go home, and lock the door behind you. In fact, that's probably why I've spent my life playing mentor to guys more interesting than myself; guys I knew were bursting with talent, who I kept pushing forward. . . . I must have unconsciously suggested some course of action to you that I knew I could never undertake myself, precisely because I didn't have the guts. Just now, you mentioned that guy Lemieux. Maybe I wasn't in love with him, after all. Maybe I was in love with his talent! Like I was in love with yours! When I listen to his records, and when I see you act on television or in the theatre, I tell myself there's a tiny part of me that lives through you. It's my only hope. There's a tiny part of me without any guts that you've managed to transpose and transcend, which means there's a bit of me I can recognize, in what you do. The way you raise your eyebrows when you speak, that's me, and the way he used the word ''profoundly'' again and again in his songs. . . . At least that's something I've done. Even if that's all. But it's hard. Because it's not enough. And it's unjust! You see, I'd like to be leaving some trace, some stamp, some mark behind me, too. I'd like to leave some indelible mark on the world, whereas in fact nobody will remember me, they'll just remember my "disciples"—as you so snidely refer to them, since you're one yourself! What a second-rate teacher you'll have had.

Silence.

When I'm shaving in the morning, and my eyes accidentally meet their reflection in the mirror, there's one terrifying word that comes into my mind, and I stand there, rooted to the spot, for a few seconds, before I can forget it. Though I'll have to face up to it one day. Perhaps by telling you, I'll be able to accept it myself.

Long silence.

Mediocrity.

LUC takes a swig of cognac and hands the glass to JEAN-MARC.

When I was a kid, I didn't want to be a writer, I wanted to be an actor. In the movies. Not because I wanted to play other characters—I didn't even understand what that meant—but because I wanted to get away from school, which I loathed, and from my family, who were stifling. Whenever a specially difficult moment occurred in the life of the secretive, sensitive child I was, I'd resort to a game I'd invented that put me into a state of wild exaltation and I'd forget everything. I'd imagine a camera following me everywhere, recording my every movement and gradually projecting the image inside my head. If I had an errand to do, or a specially difficult exam to write, I'd say to myself, "Roll the camera!" and I could see myself in the distance, coming along the street, or sitting at my desk, stuck at some arithmetic problem, then everything would become so much more interesting because it was all happening on a screen. Some of the worst moments of my childhood I managed to get through by watching myself on an imaginary screen, playing my own role in an endless adventure film. Today, I try to do the same thing sometimes, but of course, it doesn't work. Perhaps because I met you and I now know what it is to be an actor. Whenever I try to recapture that state of grace which once did wonders for me, it's you I see, playing my role, and I ask myself, why on earth did you agree to play such a dreary character?

LUC:

My God. And I came here for consolation. . . . *smiling a little, trying to change the subject* Well, if you're feeling paranoid about your lover's talents, just remember, Natasha's the last person you need worry about.

JEAN-MARC:

Don't try to change the subject Luc, it's hard enough as it is.

LUC:

You've always been inclined towards self-pity, and when you start skating on that ice, I don't know how to keep you from falling through, so I make jokes. If you've made up your mind that you're mediocre, there's probably nothing I can do, and that's sad. You won't believe me no matter what I say. If I try to convince you of the opposite, you'll gleefully demolish my arguments, one by one. You'll underline their weaknesses, their lack of maturity. As usual, it'll end up in a contest to see who's got more intellectual staying power, and as usual you'll win because you're smarter than I am, and always have been. You were winning arguments in the cradle, for Chrissake! So don't start trying to convince me you're more mediocre than I am, because if we start one of those battles, we'll regret it, and we won't feel like seeing each other for a long time.

43

JEAN-MARC:

I don't want to start a fight! I'm only telling you things I've just discovered myself, that I've never told anyone before! Paul is too young—or, in any case, he's not mature enough to understand these things. And as for my "colleagues", they're probably in the same situation as myself. I'm talking to you, Luc, for the same reasons you came to see me this evening! You and I, we can only confide in each other. I'm groping, just like you. Like you I hesitate, ask myself a thousand questions! Until now I considered my life a relative success. Though I was doing a job I liked more or less, I always tried to have a second occupation, more gratifying, more prestigious, but I couldn't manage it. What I did manage was to bring out in others what was lacking in myself—talent! It's hard, you know! It's no joke when you look at yourself in the mirror, one morning, and suddenly it hits you: you've got no talent whatsoever. It's monstrous, I tell you, it creates so many problems for me, because here I am, at the halfway point in my life, and maybe, just maybe, I don't *want* the second half to be the same as the first!

LUC:

Just what is it you want me to say? That it's true you're mediocre? I don't think so. I never thought so and I never will.   *more softly*   Let's talk about something else, Jean-Marc, we're getting into stuff that doesn't smell too good.

Silence.

JEAN-MARC:
> It's true, when you think of it, the confessional only
> works one way. Everyone who comes to me, friends as
> well as students, to pour out their troubles, their
> gripes, their bile, all those wonderful people who look
> at me with imploring eyes, begging for help—
> whenever I broach my own problems they stiffen and
> hide their faces in their hands. Can you understand
> that? Why is it that when all of you come to see me,
> it's called a cry for help, and when I go to see you, it's
> called self-pity?

LUC: *softly*
> I admire you, Jean-Marc, but if you're determined to
> prove your mediocrity to me, I'm afraid you might
> succeed, though I'm gonna do everything I can to
> prevent it, because I don't believe it's true.

> *Silence. They look at each other for a long time.*

JEAN-MARC:
> It's okay.　　　*smiling sadly*　　　You see how reasonable
> I am!

LUC:

> We ought to speak louder. I get the feeling Natasha's
> just taken out the carving knife!

> *Short silence.*

> It's so easy to make jokes about him.

JEAN-MARC:
> So what else is new. . . .

LUC:

But I can't help myself.

Silence.

He's so ridiculous. How do you manage?

JEAN-MARC:

When I go back upstairs, shortly, two big blue eyes
will be waiting for me anxiously, and I shall reassure
them with a smile. A troubled heart will sigh with
relief, arms will open wide, and I'll forget everything
that's happened down here—for a while at least.

He wipes his forehead with his hand.

If you don't want me to talk about mediocrity, Luc,
don't ask me any more questions.

Short silence.

LUC:

I just don't know what to do when you're like this . . .
I feel like running away. Anyway, I'll be going soon.
. . . I want to stop by the hospital before I go to bed,
and I've got a rehearsal in the morning.

JEAN-MARC:

"Le Chandelier"?

LUC:

No. It's for the series.

JEAN-MARC:

You look so dejected when you say that. . . .

LUC:

With reason, don't you think?

JEAN-MARC:

> When you signed your contract last year, you told me
> it would make you a very good living. It would give
> you the freedom to do what you want in the
> theatre. . . .

LUC:

> Ah, yes. The eternal excuse. We must earn our bread
> and butter. I just didn't know how bad it would be.
> The project was interesting at first, everybody was
> excited. But now that I'm in it up to the eyeballs, I
> find it dreary beyond belief.

JEAN-MARC:

> The public likes it. And it's making you famous!

LUC:

> Oh yeah. The public likes it and it's making me
> famous! Discovered at thirty-two.   *quietly*   If you
> don't want to hear any more about my problems,
> Jean-Marc, I should be on my way.

JEAN-MARC:

> You don't have to, it's okay. Actually, I watch you
> making a fool of yourself every week, and I think to
> myself you must be really unhappy. But you never talk
> about it.

LUC:

> That's because it frightens me. It's serious, you know.
> I've heard of television actors who get confused by the
> public with the characters they play, but I never
> thought it could go this far. For ten years, I did things
> all over the place; some were good, at times some were
> even excellent, but I always had the impression that
> nobody knew I existed. A year ago, the public knew
> me no better than when I came out of the Theatre
> School. Then all of a sudden, I start playing this

nutcase with a lisp in a television series, a character without any consistency whatsoever, and the public, the whole goddamn lot of them, falls head over heels in love with me! The kids imitate me so well teachers are accusing me of wanting to turn Quebec into a nation of lispers. At first I used to like being stopped on the street and in the metro, but I soon discovered nobody knew my real name, they were confusing me with that idiot character! It's incredible. When I answer people without lisping they practically fall off the sidewalk, they're so disappointed! More and more that character's taking over my life, even my identity, and I can't stand it!

Silence.

Jean-Marc, I'm on the verge of believing that the public is stupid and I don't want to believe that.

Silence.

JEAN-MARC:
Those are generalizations, Luc.

LUC:
It's hard to avoid them when every day people are calling you by a name that doesn't belong to you. The letters and phone calls I get are so pitiful, you wouldn't believe it! Declarations of love, marriage proposals, girls sending me porno shots, trying to make dates! There's even an old elocution teacher who wants to give me lessons to cure me of my lisp! I'm seriously thinking of packing it in, it's gotten so bad. When I go on stage as Fortunio at the Quat'Sous, are people gonna point to me and say: "Wowww! Get a load of that outfit!" And when I start speaking Parisian French, will they be rolling in the aisles? I know I'm exaggerating, but it terrifies me. It makes me wonder

why doesn't actor who enjoys desperate indiscriminate fucking enjoy clowning in public? And its rich variety? Different streets is an obsession for delight which is insincere?

why we chase after success. Is that what it is, success? Do people really like it? It won't be me playing Fortunio, but the guy with the lisp. I didn't become an actor to get stuck in one role! And a bad one, at that! Am I going to die saying, "For heaven'th thake, for heaven'th thake, women are jutht impothible!" like I do every week in closeup for millions of giggling spectators? I play a deathly boring character in a deathly boring series and people can't get enough of it! When we come in for rehearsal Monday morning, the whole gang of us can hardly believe the asinine things we have to say. We change the lines we find really obnoxious, we make cuts, we do everything we can to improve it, but even then, what we end up with is a pile of shit! But it's a hit! That too is mediocrity, Jean-Marc! Collective, consenting mediocrity! Which is much worse! We flatter the basest instincts of the people who watch us, we make the coarsest jokes, not exactly spelling it out, but painfully obvious, and we shoot to the top of the popularity charts. There are some programmes other than ours that try to educate people a bit, but almost no one watches them, because they're not funny. I'm not against making people laugh, or simply entertaining them, but I want it to mean something! And I want the public to distinguish between *me*, the person I am, and the person I play! I'm tired of covering up, beating around the bush, telling little white lies every time I'm interviewed. I'm sick of talking to journalists who know very well I'm gay, yet persist in asking me about the women in my life! Most of all, I'm sick of people believing I'm really in love with the actress who plays my girlfriend. And so is she! Sometimes I feel like calling a press conference and once and for all declaring that I'm homosexual. That'd solve the problem!

JEAN-MARC:
Your private life is no one else's business.

49

LUC:
> Not true, I'm afraid. All the time I was a struggling
> unknown actor, I had a private life that was no one
> else's business; but now that I'm in demand
> everywhere, I can't stand the pretense, the pack of lies
> I have to tell over and over again. I don't want to be a
> hero, I don't want to carry a flag. I just want people to
> take me for what I am—if they're interested. I want
> people to say I act well. I want them to say I look
> good, because I'm an actor, and an actor's an
> exhibitionist. That's it: I *want* people to take me for an
> actor! Not a character. And perhaps that's the only
> way I can do it. Some fucked-up producers might
> never want to hear of me again, and no doubt a lot of
> my fans would be traumatized, but at least everything
> would be clear.

JEAN-MARC:
> If I wanted to be mean, I'd say there's a fair chance
> you'd still get the same amount of mail, only it'd be
> slightly different . . .

LUC:
> I've thought about that. I can handle my own kind
> alright. What I can't handle is women who don't know
> I'm gay. In my own circle there's no problem,
> everyone knows it, and for our kind, it's a privileged
> milieu. But I don't want to deceive people who believe
> everything they're told, who end up taking me for
> some kind of Romeo just because for the past year or
> so they've seen me with my arms around the most
> beautiful girls in Montreal.

JEAN-MARC:
> I thought you said they were stupid.

LUC:

> Sometimes I think they are, but that's no reason to
> take advantage of them. I'd rather have somebody
> abuse me on the street because he thinks I'm sick and
> abnormal than tell me how funny I am or what a nice
> guy, because he takes me for somebody who doesn't
> exist!

> *He grins.*

> And, if it costs me my "career", I'll come back and
> mark papers with you. . . .

JEAN-MARC:

> I get the feeling there's another wisecrack about
> Natasha on the way.

LUC:

> On the contrary! You see how you misjudge me!

> *Silence.*

> If, when my father dies, my name should make the
> gossip columns of the entertainment page, I want them
> to talk about *my* father, not the father of the guy with
> the lisp.

JEAN-MARC:

> That would be very brave on your part, Luc, but
> there's something I don't understand.

LUC:

> Don't tell me I'm wrong, Jean-Marc. Not you.

JEAN-MARC:

I'm not saying you're wrong, but I think your reasons
may not be the right ones. If you were straight, Luc,
you'd be stuck with the same problem of being
identified with the character you play. So how would
you escape that? Would you feel obliged to invent some
scandal so people could differentiate you from him? If
you declare to the world that you're gay, at the risk of
losing your job, your friends, your allies, it strikes me
you should be doing it out of solidarity, not just to
exorcise some character that's taking over your life.

LUC:

You know me, and causes. . . .

JEAN-MARC:

It is a cause, whether you like it or not. And you
wouldn't be able to dissociate yourself from it,
precisely because you are a public figure!

LUC:

Don't start preaching, Jean-Marc, you know I hate it!

JEAN-MARC:

Luc, if deep down inside you don't want people to
know about it, because you don't want to carry a flag,
as you say, don't say anything.

LUC:

I know there's a bunch of idiots who'd just as soon
know nothing, but surely there are people somewhere
who could take it. I can't believe there's no one.

JEAN-MARC:

>Luc, you've always advocated secrecy and marginality, what's got into you all of a sudden, to go shouting it from the rooftops? You've always been proud of being different, you always said that you needed the complicity you found in our milieu, that it stimulated you, that your creativity was nourished by it, that you couldn't function in a straight milieu, because everybody there is the same. Even when we were together, you used to laugh at "the straight little queer couples", as you called them, that you found so hopelessly boring! "Reassure me," you'd say, "Tell me we're not as boring as that." So don't start telling me now that you really want to settle for the prim and proper, aseptic and discreet household faggot who wouldn't hurt a fly, that all the world's gonna want you to become! Once you've told everyone you're gay, they're gonna want to know more. It's big news, and it'll make great gossip! When you tell me you don't want to be a hero, I believe you, but you risk becoming one all the same, and that's just not you, Luc. In three months, you won't want to hear about it, you'll be telling everyone to go screw themselves! Are you going to give them a rundown on your sexual capers, like you did me tonight? Of course not! On the contrary, you'll end up inventing a cute little boyfriend to put their minds at rest! And that too will be living a lie! An even more mediocre lie than the others.

LUC:

>Jean-Marc—you're getting me all mixed up! In any case, the worst thing that could happen to me is that they get rid of the guy with the lisp! Imagine! I'd have to go and earn my living somewhere else. In the meantime, I'm going to see my father at the hospital; first things first.

JEAN-MARC:
>That's it? The discussion's closed?

LUC:

>There's no point in us talking about it till tomorrow morning. We won't solve anything—that's what's sad.

>*Silence.*

>Perhaps you're right again, Jean-Marc, it's maddening. Ah! But wait a minute, you're not right! The world out there is gonna know about it, and if they don't like it, they can shove it! If it's too much for them I can always disappear and become a marginal, misunderstood actor once again, who knows what he wants and doesn't give a damn if he ends up in the "has beens" column! "Remember the actor who played the guy with the lisp on television, a few years ago? He's a waiter in a bar!" That's right! A waiter in a bar making five hundred bucks a week taking no one for a ride, and he's telling you all to go screw yourselves! Well, right now, I feel like telling them to shove it! . . . I love it passionately, Jean-Marc, being an actor. It's my whole life, but Christ, I hate to fuck people over! If I can't avoid that, just give me the strength to retire with dignity before I have too much to reproach myself for. I'm going to play Fortunio soon. . . . It's one of my greatest dreams, and I must do it now while I'm still an ingenue . . . Before long it won't be possible. But it mustn't be a circus act that people come to see for the wrong reasons! I want them to come and see *me, me* playing in de Musset. Here we go. I knew this was gonna happen!

JEAN-MARC:
>What?

LUC:
>I'm gonna cry. I think I'm gonna cry.

Now JEAN-MARC also gets up and goes and sits in the armchair where LUC has been sitting. LUC comes and kneels down next to JEAN-MARC.

Help me! Tell me a story like you did when I used to get depressed. Pretend you're my father one last time. When he's dead, I won't ask you again.

During the whole of JEAN-MARC's story, LUC weeps silently, arms folded, his body bent forward. JEAN-MARC speaks slowly, very tenderly, as if he were really addressing a very small boy.

JEAN-MARC:
Once upon a time there was a little boy who was ashamed of his father because his father hadn't gone to school for very long and he didn't know very much. And also, the little boy's father would speak very loud in the streetcar, because there were still streetcars in those days, and that made the little boy very embarrassed and he would blush, and he would even pretend he didn't know this great big man who was waving his arms and talking so loud to everybody, and whistling when he had nothing more to say. You see, during his first years at school, his father would help him do his homework every night, and the little boy was very happy, but at the end of his third year, his father had taken him aside and said to him: "This is where I stop, son. I can't keep up with you any more. You'll have to go on alone now." And the little boy felt very ashamed. But the father realized it, and to win back his son's admiration, he took him by the hand one fine Saturday morning and took him to the new Steinberg's, brand new, at the corner of Mount Royal and Bordeaux. And then and there, he took the little boy and he stood him in front of the row of Campbell's soups, and he said to him, "Look closely, my boy. See all the red labels on the tins of Campbell's soup there? You see the red on those labels, it's exactly

the same on every one of them, there's not one tin
that's a different red from any other. You see, it
wouldn't look nice and people would know it wasn't all
made at the same time. Now, you wanna know
something? I'm the one who prints them! In every big
city in North America there's only one pressman in
one print shop who knows the secret of Campbell's
red, and here in Montreal, that man is your father!''
And from that day on, the father grew and grew in the
little boy's estimation; he became the most important
man in the world, and sometimes, the little boy would
even take his friends or classmates and take them to
Steinberg's, and he would line them up in front of the
shelves of soup tins, and he'd say: ''You see that? It's
my father who did that! My father invented that red!''

> *LUC wipes his eyes with the palms of his hands, then
> with his shirtsleeves.*

The story never tells what became of them. The story
ends when the little boy was still a little boy and his
father was still a giant.

LUC:
> You never told me that one before. . . .

JEAN-MARC:
> I was waiting till you were ready.

LUC: *still very upset*
> I wonder where you get them, these stories.

JEAN-MARC:
> Well, that's one an old lover told me, the first night we
> spent together. . . .

LUC:
> No, not the first night.

56

JEAN-MARC:
>Yes.

LUC:
>Ah . . . I didn't remember it! . . . Well, I'm going
>now, this time for real. . . .

JEAN-MARC:
>No, don't! Stay and relax. I'll go and see your father.
>I'll go and see him on my own. There's some things
>I've been wanting to tell him for a long time.

LUC:
>Okay, I'll wait for you. I don't feel like going home
>right now.

JEAN-MARC:
>Why not? Make yourself at home. You can read
>something. And if you want to talk about it again
>when I come back . . .

LUC:
>What about Paul?

JEAN-MARC:
>He'll understand. If you were really nice, you'd go up
>and talk to him.

LUC:
>Maybe. . . .

>*JEAN-MARC hesitates before going out.*

JEAN-MARC:
>See you later. Is there anything you want to say to
>your father?

LUC: *after a moment's hesitation*
Jean-Marc . . . sometimes I feel like coming to see
you, and making a real heavy scene, worse than
tonight, and saying "Take me back. I need affection
desperately. I'm all alone. And I miss you so much."
In fact, that's what I nearly did. I know it's ridiculous
and we'd regret it bitterly after two or three days, but
the need gets stronger and stronger and more and
more frequent. Sometimes, it's almost as if what we
have between us is too controlled, and it bothers me. I
have the feeling that the years of real passion in my life
are already behind me, and will never come back. I
live on remembered smells and remembered passions
because all I feel these days is gratification, swift and
fleeting. I need it all. To be free as a bird, yet have my
daily bread. But I can't have it all. And the choice is
so difficult. Even if it's already made.

Silence.

Tell my father I'll be there tomorrow afternoon.

They look at each other and smile.

Ciao!

JEAN-MARC:
Ciao!

JEAN-MARC leaves.
LUC looks around slowly, then goes over to
JEAN-MARC's desk.
He breathes in deeply, closing his eyes.
He picks up the first paper waiting to be corrected.

LUC:
Two mistakes in the title alone. . . . Incredible!

BLACKOUT

58